Printed in the U.S.A.

ISBN 0-7172-8703-3

JIM HENSON'S MUPPETS
IN

Too Many Promises

A Book About Saying No

By Eleanor Freemont • Illustrated by Tom Brannon

GROLIER

One morning, there was a new poster on the bulletin board announcing a Make-a-Book contest. Everybody crowded around to read it. "Books must be in by May 1," Kermit read.

"Gee," said Piggy. "That's two weeks away!"

"I'm going to write a book of all the jump rope rhymes I know," said Skeeter. She skipped off to think of some. "Let's see . . . I'll start with 'A my name is Alice and I come from Alaska.'"

Gonzo was excited, too. "I know just what I'm going to call my book," he said. *"Really Great Things You Can Do with Fungus."*

That afternoon, Fozzie walked home with Kermit. "I was thinking, Kermit," he said. "Why don't we write a joke book together?"

"Uh, gee," said Kermit. "I was kind of thinking of doing a book by myself. About baseball."

"Please, please, please?" begged Fozzie.

"Oh, Fozzie, I could never say no to you," said Kermit.

That night, as Kermit was oiling his baseball mitt, the phone rang. It was Piggy.

"Hi, Kermie," said Piggy very sweetly. "You
know that book-writing contest at school?"

Kermit knew what was coming. "Y-Yes," he
said hesitantly.

"Yes? You mean you'll work with me?" she said. "Oh, Kermie, I knew you wouldn't say no. I have this great idea for a book, too. It's about a handsome prince who saves a beautiful princess from an evil queen who turns people into donkeys, and . . ."

"Piggy—" Kermit tried to say. But Piggy didn't hear him. She just kept talking.

Kermit felt confused. How could he promise Fozzie and not Piggy? Piggy's feelings would be hurt.

"Okay, I'll do it," said Kermit. "I could never say no to you, Piggy."

"Oh, Kermie, that's so wonderful!" said Piggy. "We'd better start writing soon."

So the next day they began working.

"Are you sure the prince should save the princess?" asked Kermit. "Isn't that a little, uh, old-fashioned? Maybe the princess should save the prince."

"No, no, no," said Piggy. "I know just how this book should be."

"Okay," said Kermit, sighing.

The next afternoon, Kermit met Fozzie at the library, and they began working on their joke book.

"Do we need quite so many knock-knock jokes?" asked Kermit. "We really have an awful lot of them."

"We definitely need a lot," said Fozzie firmly. "They're the best ones."

Kermit's eyes drifted over to the baseball section. All the books looked so interesting!

Boy, I could write some really good tips on throwing curveballs, thought Kermit wistfully. *If only I had the time.*

"C'mon, Kermit," said Fozzie. "Let's find some more knock-knock jokes."

That night, Kermit got home and ate dinner so late that he had to do his homework under the covers with a flashlight.

For a whole week, Kermit's life went on in this way. One afternoon he'd work with Fozzie. The next afternoon he'd work with Piggy. Kermit didn't have time to do his homework. He didn't have time to play baseball. Saddest of all, he didn't have time to work on his how-to-throw-a-curveball book.

WHO'S THERE?

On Friday afternoon, a week before the contest deadline, Kermit hurried to the school bus. He wanted to get home to do his homework.

Fozzie sat down next to him.

"Kermit," he said, "we still need more knock-knock jokes. Maybe we should work on our book this afternoon."

Piggy was sitting in front of them. "Hold on, Kermit," she said. "You can't be working on a book with Fozzie! You have to come over to my house and work on our book!"

"I'm sorry, Piggy," said Fozzie. "You must be mistaken. Kermit is working with me."

Kermit stood up. Then he remembered he wasn't supposed to stand up on the school bus. So he sat down with a plop.

"Wait a second!" he yelled. "I can't do this anymore!"

Fozzie and Piggy looked at him, stunned.

"I know I said yes to both of you," Kermit said, "but I never should have. I'm a wreck! Besides, you both know what you want your books to be like. You don't need me. I'm really sorry, but it's time I started saying no!"

"Gee," said Fozzie. "I didn't know you were feeling that way. I wish you had said no to start with. It would have been okay with me."

"Thanks, Fozzie," said Kermit.

"I can finish the book by myself," Fozzie went on. "I'm having fun looking for knock-knock jokes."

"Maybe you shouldn't have said yes to me, either," said Piggy, "but it's okay. I can finish the book alone. Besides, I still think the prince should rescue the princess."

"Thanks, you guys," said Kermit. He sighed
in relief. "I feel like I just unloaded a ton of
bricks."

"So, Kermit," said Fozzie, "do you think you
can write your baseball book in a week?"

"I'm going to try!" said Kermit with a grin.

When Kermit got home, he did his homework. Then he started working on his book.

"A good curveball," he began, "is just a matter of practice—and a little magic." He was very pleased with his first sentence. From then on, he worked on his book every day.

On the morning of May 1, Kermit walked to school with Fozzie and Piggy. "Did you finish your book?" asked Fozzie.

"I've got it right here," replied Kermit, patting his book bag.

"I've got mine, too," said Piggy proudly.

"So do I," said Fozzie.

"Well, good luck to all of us," said Kermit.

The three of them shook hands.

At last the awards day came. A special assembly was called to announce the winner.

"We had a hard time choosing," said Mr. Bumper. "But there was one book that was just so . . . interesting, we had to award it first prize. The book was *Really Great Things You Can Do with Fungus*. Congratulations, Gonzo!"

"We teachers learned a lot from the books you all wrote," said Mr. Bumper as he pinned on Gonzo's ribbon.

"I sure learned a lot about stuff you can do with fungus," said Gonzo happily.

And I learned a lot, too, thought Kermit. *About curveballs—and about saying no!*